For Peter and Laura,
and their prizewinning pup,
Huckleberry!
—A.S.C.

HarperCollins®, ■®, and I Can Read Book® are trademarks of HarperCollins Publishers Inc.

Library of Congress Cataloging-in-Publication Data

Capucilli, Alyssa Satin

Biscuit wins a prize / story by Alyssa Satin Capucilli ; pictures by Pat Schories.

p. cm. — (My first I can read book)

Summary: Biscuit, a small puppy, gets excited when he is entered in a pet show.

ISBN-10: 0-06-009455-9 (trade bdg.) — ISBN-13: 978-0-06-009455-3 (trade bdg.)

ISBN-10: 0-06-009457-5 (lib. bdg.) — ISBN-13: 978-0-06-009457-7 (lib. bdg.)

ISBN-10: 0-06-009458-3 (pbk.) — ISBN-13: 978-0-06-009458-4 (pbk.)

[1. Dogs—Fiction. 2. Pet shows—Fiction.] I. Schories, Pat, ill. II. Title. III. Series.

PZ7.C179Bitc 2004

[E]—dc21

2002154809

CIP

AC

17 18 SCP 15 14

❖

I Can Read!

SHARED My First READING

Biscuit
Wins a Prize

story by ALYSSA SATIN CAPUCILLI
pictures by PAT SCHORIES

HarperCollins*Publishers*

Here, Biscuit.

It's time for the pet show!

Woof, woof!

There will be lots of pets,
and prizes, too!
Woof, woof!

Come along, sweet puppy.
You want to look your best.
Woof!

Hold still, Biscuit.

Woof, woof!

Funny puppy! Don't tug now!

Hold still, Biscuit.

Woof, woof!

Oh, Biscuit!

It's not time to roll over.

Woof, woof!

It's time for the pet show!

Look at all the pets, Biscuit.

Woof, woof!

Biscuit sees his friend Puddles.

Bow wow!
Woof, woof!

Biscuit sees his friend Sam.

Ruff!

Woof, woof!

Biscuit sees
lots of new friends, too.

Woof, woof!

Hold still now, Biscuit.

Here comes the judge.

Woof!

Oh no, Biscuit. Come back!

Biscuit wants
to see the fish.
Woof!

Biscuit wants
to see the bunnies.
Woof!

Woof, woof!

Biscuit wants
to see all of the pets
at the pet show!

Silly puppy! Here you are.

What prize will you win now?
Woof, woof!

Oh, Biscuit!

You won the best prize of all!

Woof!